Elaine,
You're a Brat!

23

Elaine,
You're a Brat!

Malorie Blackman

Illustrated by Doffy Weir

ORCHARD BOOKS

ORCHARD BOOKS
96 Leonard Street, London EC2A 4RH

Orchard Books Australia
14 Mars Road, Lane Cove, NSW 2066

ISBN 1 85213 642 1 (paperback)
ISBN 1 85213 365 1 (hardback)

First published in Great Britain 1991
First paperback publication 1994

A CIP catalogue record for this book is available
from the British Library.

Printed in Great Britain

To Neil, with love,
and
to Aunt Millie and Uncle George

Contents

1

I Don't Want To

ELAINE GLARED OUT OF THE CAR window at her granma's house. It was horrible. It was big and spooky and Elaine didn't want to stay there – no she didn't!

She lay down on her stomach on the back seat and started kicking and punching and yelling and screaming.

"I don't want to stay with Granma. I DON'T WANT TO!" Elaine shouted.

"But Elaine, it's only for a few weeks. You know I would take you with me if I could, but I can't," Elaine's dad pleaded.

"What seems to be the problem?"

Elaine lifted her head at the sound of Granma's voice. She didn't like Granma. Granma had black hair streaked with silver-white strands and wore a peach-coloured dress that was all ruffles and bows. She had old-fashioned half-moon

spectacles perched low down on her nose but she looked over them rather than through them with her round, piercing brown eyes.

"I won't stay with her, I won't," Elaine shouted. "She's dumpy and frumpy."

"Elaine! That is no way to talk about your granma," Dad said sternly.

"Elaine dear, you're just in time for dinner. And it's all your favourites," Granma smiled.

"You don't know what my favourites are," Elaine said suspiciously.

"Yes, I do. You like sausages and chips and baked beans followed by vanilla ice-cream and chocolate sauce."

Elaine thought hard.

"All right then. I'll get out of the car . . . but only because I'm hungry," she said at last.

"Wave goodbye to your father," Granma said.

"I won't," Elaine said. "He won't take me with him."

Elaine walked towards the house and didn't look back at her dad once. Granma watched Elaine and frowned.

Elaine felt alone and miserable, utterly miserable. Her dad was the International Development Manager for a large company that made computers and he was always jetting off here, there and everywhere. Occasionally – very occasionally – he took Elaine with him, but more often he didn't. Dad never seemed to spend longer than a few months in any one place.

As a result Elaine had lived in more houses and been to more schools than any eight people put together. And because she had been to so many schools, Elaine didn't have any close friends. She hadn't been in one school long enough to make any.

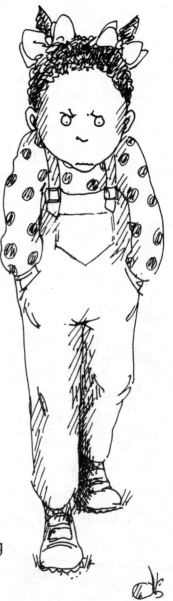

Elaine felt like an unwanted parcel, being shunted back and forth between teachers and boring aunts and even some of Dad's friends, none of whom really wanted her.

"It's not fair." Elaine kicked a stone as she walked towards Granma's house.

Now her dad had dumped her on her granma who didn't want her any more than anyone else did. There'd be no one to play with, nothing to see, nothing to do. And Elaine would have to put up with tons and tons of nothing for a whole *month* until she started yet another school in September.

"I hate school, I hate this house, I hate EVERYTHING," Elaine said, so fiercely that her eyes narrowed into thin slits and her lips turned down in a severe pout.

"I wish . . . I wish I could find someone who wanted to be friends with *me*, just me," Elaine whispered.

"Come along, Elaine," Granma said, appearing from nowhere. "I've just got time to show you around my home as you've never stayed here for longer than lunch before."

And so Granma and Elaine wandered all around the huge house before dinner. Elaine sulked in the basement, tutted in the living-room, pouted in the bedrooms and sighed in the attic.

"I don't want to do this any more," Elaine said. "I want my dinner please."

"Very well then," Granma said and off they went to the dining-room.

But Elaine missed Granma's frown as Granma followed her up the stairs.

2

It's Been on the Floor!

THE DINING-ROOM WAS ON THE FIRST floor, overlooking the back garden. The sun had almost set so Granma had to put on the light. Elaine sat down for her dinner and she wasn't pleased. No, she wasn't!

"This sausage is too small and the beans shouldn't be touching the chips – now the chips will be all soggy. And these beans are all clumped together. Yuk!" Elaine moaned.

"It tastes lovely," Granma said, tucking into her dinner. "Just try some."

Elaine glared down at her dinner plate. She took her fork and started stirring her food round and round until it was one big, multi-coloured blob on her plate.

"Don't play with your dinner, Elaine," Granma said.

"I don't want these smelly beans," Elaine said sullenly.

"And I'm sure they don't want you either," Granma said calmly, "But you'll still have to eat them."

"And I don't want these stinky chips," Elaine sulked. "And I don't want this tiny, teeny-weeny, rotten sausage."

Granma bent down to tickle her black cat Jolly behind its ears.

"Pretty Jolly, good Jolly. You'd eat your dinner, wouldn't you?" Granma murmured.

Elaine picked up her plate whilst Granma wasn't looking. Could she do it . . .? Should she do it . . .?

"Jolly, I'm beginning to think Elaine is quite a little madam?" Granma said, still not looking up.

19

'This will show Gran!' Elaine smirked silently.

She lifted up Granma's lace tablecloth and flung everything on her plate under the table.

"You're a good cat aren't you, Jolly," Granma said, stilll stroking Jolly's neck. "You wouldn't throw your food on my good carpet like some others I know."

Elaine stared in amazement at Granma. How had Granma known that Elaine had thrown her food on the floor? The lace tablecloth reached down to the carpet. Granma couldn't have seen her ... could she?

"I'm not going to pick it up." Elaine folded her arms across her chest.

Granma straightened up.

"Pick what up, dear?" Granma asked.

"My dinner."

"Pick it up from where, dear?"

"The floor," Elaine said impatiently.

"But your dinner isn't on the floor, dear," Granma said, prodding a chip with her fork and popping it in her mouth. "Look for yourself if you don't believe me."

Elaine looked down at her plate. It was empty. She bent over and lifted up the tablecloth. The sausage, the chips and every single baked bean – they had all vanished.

Elaine straightened up again.

"Well it *was* . . ." Elaine stopped speaking as she stared down at the plate before her.

Her food was now back on the plate! Elaine blinked twice, hard. She had to be

imagining things. She lifted up the tablecloth and looked under it again. Then she
looked back at the dinner table. The chips,
the beans, the sausage, they were definitely
back on her plate.

"How . . . how did you do that?" Elaine
asked, astounded. "I threw my dinner
under the table."

Elaine frowned down at her plate.
Granma couldn't have picked up everything off the floor *that* fast.

"I'm still not eating it," Elaine said. "It's been on the floor."

Granma looked at Elaine very carefully.

"My dear," Granma said at last, "I've met some bad-mannered, unpleasant characters in my time – I really have. Like that dreadful dragon who decided to live at the bottom of my garden and frightened all the birds away. And that nasty, greedy troll who tried to eat me because I beat him at chess. But after due consideration I have decided that you are the rudest, most spoilt, most disagreeable child I have ever met. In short Elaine, you're a brat!"

"Does that mean you're sending me back home to Dad?" Elaine said hopefully.

"No, it does not," Granma replied.

Granma frowned down at Jolly.

"Jolly, what should I do to teach this young madam a lesson?" Granma asked.

"Miaow! Miaow!" Jolly replied.

"Jolly's just an ugly, stupid cat," Elaine snapped. "She's as frumpy and dumpy as you are . . ."

"That does it," Granma interrupted. "My girl, I'm going to teach you a lesson you'll never forget."

3

Elaine the Cat

ELAINE SPRANG OUT OF HER CHAIR. She wasn't frightened, not at all. Granma stood up slowly and pointed at Elaine.

"Since you think Jolly's so ugly and stupid you will switch with Jolly. You will live in Jolly's body and Jolly will live in yours. And I won't change you back until..." Granma's eyes suddenly gleamed. "Until you find my wedding ring which I

lost years ago and until you've learnt some manners."

"Don't talk wet!" Elaine laughed.

But then something very strange happened.

Lightning flashed and thunder crashed *inside* the dining-room. Suddenly the room went dark. Elaine looked around, frightened.

Then the light was on again and everything was still.

"There! It's done! How does it feel to be a girl, Jolly!" Granma said.

Elaine stared up at the girl above her.

It *was* her!

There she was sitting at the dinner table – only it wasn't her because how could she be watching herself? What was going on? Elaine looked down at her hands and stared so hard she was surprised her eyes didn't pop out of her head and plop out onto the

carpet. Her hands had
disappeared. Instead
she had . . . paws.

Paws covered with thick, black fur which
shone like her hair when she'd just washed
it. Elaine stretched around to look at her
feet. More paws! And covered in the same
black fur.

What was happening?

"Jump up on the cupboard and look in the mirror above it if you want to see what you look like," Granma said, looking down at her.

Elaine wondered why Granma was suddenly so tall. Elaine began to walk over to the cupboard but she stopped abruptly. It felt as if she was walking on all fours. Elaine started walking again until she was just in front of the cupboard. The top of the cupboard somehow looked very far away. Before it had been just shorter than her head. Elaine looked up at it. She sat back and sprang up knowing that she *could* jump that high. Once she was on top of the cupboard she looked in the mirror on the wall before her.

"I'm a cat!" Elaine shrieked.

There in the mirror, staring back at her was the face of Jolly, only now it was her face.

"I said I'd switch you with Jolly," Granma said, walking up to her. "If this doesn't teach you some manners I don't know what will."

"You've turned me into a cat!" Elaine shrieked again.

"I have not. You're just in Jolly's body, that's all. Your body's over here with Jolly in it.

Elaine the cat turned around to see Jolly sitting at the table.

"Miaow! I like being a girrrrl!" Jolly said before bending her head to lick at the baked beans on Elaine's plate.

"Even though Jolly's in your body she's

29

still got cat habits," Granma sighed. "Never mind. At least she can keep me company and she won't be as rude as you."

"I'm sorry, Granma. Please change me back," Elaine pleaded. "I won't do it again."

"I can't change you back," Granma shrugged. "Not until you find my wedding ring and what's more you've only got until dinner-time tomorrow to find it. I forgot that the switch trick has a time limit."

"But what happens if I don't find it?" Elaine asked.

"Then you'll have to remain a cat forever."

"But Granma . . ." Elaine begged.

"It's your own fault." Granma wagged a finger at Elaine. "You shouldn't have made me lose my temper. Now you'd better start searching for my wedding ring – unless of course you *like* being a cat."

No, Elaine didn't like being a cat – not at all. No, she didn't! She wanted to be a girl again.

Elaine jumped down from the cupboard and ran out of the dining-room. She'd find Granma's ring if it was the last thing she did.

4

Grimbledon Scunacrunch

ELAINE THE CAT RAN ALONG THE landing which was filled with low lights and long shadows.

"I'm a cat," she wailed, "I'm a cat!"

Elaine glanced down at her paws and wailed even louder. She didn't like being furry!

"What am I going to do now?" Elaine thought unhappily.

She'd have to find Granma's ring if she

ever wanted to be a girl again. Elaine was just about to turn the corner to go up the stairs when she skidded to a halt. There, on the opposite wall, was the huge shadow of some mega-enormous beast. There was something around the corner waiting for her . . .

It had huge legs and a long back and an even longer tail.

"Who . . . who's there?" Elaine called out, terrified.

A loud, deep voice from around the corner replied,

"*My name is Grimbledon Scunacrunch*
  I can eat a rhino for my lunch,
  I'm big and bad and bold and keen,
  The meanest beast you've EVER seen!"

Elaine looked up and down the landing. She *had* to go around the corner. That was the only way to the attic and that's where she wanted to start searching for Granma's wedding ring. Elaine stared at the long shadow on the wall before her. She couldn't sit there forever, not going anywhere. Elaine took a deep breath.

"I'm not afraid of you – whoever you are," She called out.

Elaine almost couldn't hear herself over the noise of her knees knocking together, and now that she had four knees they made a great deal more noise than two.

Holding her head high, she walked slowly but steadily around the corner.

"Arrgh! Jolly the ginormous! I didn't recognise your voice. I've had it now."

Elaine looked down to where the voice was coming from.

"Who are you?" she asked, surprised.

"Grimbledon Scunacrunch the seventy-fifth – at your service!"

"But you're a mouse!"

"Of course I'm a mouse. Go on Jolly you fiend, get it over with. Don't toy with me! Knock me block off!" Grimbledon closed his eyes and stuck out his neck.

Elaine frowned. "Why on earth would I do that?" she asked.

Grimbledon opened his eyes and stared at her without saying a word.

"Was it *you* who made that giant shadow?" Elaine raised a paw to point at the wall.

"I did," Grimbledon said slowly. "I make the biggest, boldest shadow don't you think?"

"Yes I do. It's very impressive, especially for a mouse. I thought you were at least as big as an elephant," Elaine said, even more amazed.

Grimbledon regarded Elaine thoughtfully.

"Who are you? You look like Jolly the devious but you don't sound like her. And you're not very smart are you? Mind you I've never met a cat who was smart. Sly yes, smart no."

"I'm not a cat. I'm a girl," Elaine said indignantly.

"Does that mean you're not going to eat me," Grimbledon asked hopefully.

"Ugh! No fear!" Elaine shivered at the thought.

Grimbledon breathed a sigh of relief. "Now I *know* you're not Jolly the sly. Jolly the underhand would have swallowed me whole in two seconds flat. So tell me how you came to look like Jolly the nasty."

"Granma put me in Jolly's body because I . . . I threw my food on the floor." Elaine felt very silly saying it.

"Why did you do that?" Grimbledon asked politely.

"I didn't want it." Elaine pouted.

"Why didn't you just say that you didn't want it?"

"Because I . . . I . . . just didn't."

"You're not very smart are you? Are you sure you're not a cat?" Grimbledon queried.

"My name is Elaine and I'm a girl, I promise. Only I'll never be a girl again if I don't find Granma's wedding ring by this time tomorrow."

"Where did your gran lose it?" Grimbledon asked.

"If she knew that she'd know where to find it and then it wouldn't be lost," Elaine said crossly.

"Hhmm! Excuse me I'm sure," Grimbledon said, peeved, "I was only trying to blinkin' help."

With a toss of his head, Grimbledon turned and began to walk off.

"No! Don't go. I . . . I need your help. I'm sorry I was rude," Elaine mumbled. She wasn't used to apologising but she realised that both of them working together would find the ring faster than just Elaine looking by herself. And it would be nice to have someone to talk to whilst she was searching.

"Let me get this straight," Grimbledon said. "If I help you then your gran will switch you back so that you'll be a girl again and Jolly the dunderhead will be a cat again."

"That's right," Elaine said eagerly.

"I'm not sure I want Jolly back." Grimbledon frowned.

"Does that mean you won't help me?" Elaine asked.

Grimbledon smiled. "Of course I'll help you. I'd do anything to get back at Jolly the poisonous. I bet she just loves being a girl."

"Well, that's what she said before I left the room," Elaine remembered.

"That clinches it. All right then," Grimbledon said briskly, "let's find your gran's ring."

5

Vinegar Blunderthud

"WHERE SHOULD WE START?" ELAINE asked. "I was going to work my way down from the attic to the basement."

"Blinkin' good idea," said Grimbledon.

So Elaine the cat and Grimbledon Scunacrunch the mouse both scampered up to the attic. The attic was dark and dingy and full of cobwebs. The only light came from the moon trying to shine in at the skylight way above them.

"It'll take all year to find Granma's ring in this jumble," said Elaine, padding through the open attic door.

"Not if we have a plan. I make the biggest, best plans in the world," said Grimbledon modestly. "Why don't we . . . "

"Please wipe your feet," a squeaky voice ordered suddenly. "What a distinct lack of manners."

"Who's there?" Elaine called out, looking every which way to see who was speaking.

"PLEASE WIPE YOUR FEET!" the squeaky voice was much louder this time. "I go to a great deal of trouble and effort to keep this attic in tip-top, minty-flinty condition and you two just wander in here without . . . "

"All right, all right," Grimbledon interrupted. "Look I'm wiping my four feet – *see*."

"And I'm wiping *my* four feet," Elaine said, wiping one paw after the other. "Although I don't really see why. This attic is grubby and grimy and full of yukky-icky cobwebs . . . "

"GRUBBY . . . GRIMY . . . CO . . . CO . . . COBWEBS!" The squeaky voice spluttered and squealed.

Elaine and Grimbledon heard the patter and scurry of lots of tiny feet heading straight towards them.

"I'll have you know that what you so rudely call cobwebs are in fact the best silk tapestries. Cobwebs are old and falling apart. If you bothered to look closely you would see that each work of art in this attic is *new* and woven with care and skill, patience and artistry, love and . . . "

"All right, all right. We get the idea," Grimbledon interrupted.

"Hhmm! Hhmm!" said the sulky spider

who stood before them waving four arms in the air whilst balancing on her other four legs.

"I'm sorry. We didn't mean to upset you," Elaine said.

"Cobwebs indeed! What nerve! What cheek!"

"I'm Elaine," Elaine interrupted hastily. "I'm a girl really but my granma switched me with Jolly the cat, so now Jolly is in my body and I'm in hers."

"I'm Vinegar," sniffed the spider, "Vinegar Blunderthud."

"And I'm Grimbledon Scunacrunch." The mouse bowed low. "I'm Elaine's friend."

"Are you?" Elaine asked surprised. "Are you really my friend?"

"Of course I am." Grimbledon smiled.

Elaine grinned at him. "Thanks Grimbledon," she said. "I've never had a real friend before."

"That's all very well my dear, but we're

wandering off the point," said Vinegar. "How long must you remain in Jolly the detestable's body?"

"Until I find Granma's ring," Elaine explained.

"You must help us," Grimbledon said anxiously. "Jolly the nasty likes being a girl and right this minute she's having a good time at Elaine's expense."

"That's why we're up here," Elaine said. "We're looking for my granma's ring. If I don't find it by tomorrow dinner-time then I'll be a cat forever and Jolly will be a girl forever."

"As a cat, you're a vast improvement on Jolly the vile if I may say so," said Vinegar.

"Thank you," Elaine said sadly. "But I don't want to stay a cat. I want to be a girl again. Will . . . will you help us?"

"Of course I'll help," Vinegar said. "I don't like Jolly the unpleasant either. She'll

be even more unbearable as a girl than she was as a cat. But first things first. I would suggest that our next step is to get some help for the search. Grimbledon, are some of your friends in the house?" Vinegar asked.

"One or two," Grimbledon replied.

"Will they help us?" Vinegar asked.

"If I ask them," Grimbledon said.

"And I'll ask my friends," Vinegar said. "That way we're more likely to find the ring sooner rather than later."

47

"It's . . . it's very kind of both of you,' Elaine whispered. "I don't know what I would do without your help."

"Don't mention it, dear, don't mention it. Anyone who doesn't care for Jolly the foul is a friend of mine. That cat is rude and disagreeable and never thinks of anyone but herself."

Elaine could feel her face burning. A lot of people thought that she was rude and disagreeable too.

"Let's both call our friends. After you, Grimbledon."

"Oh no! After you," Grimbledon said.

"Thank you. So kind. So courteous," said Vinegar.

Then she whistled three times – high, delicate, piercing whistles that passed straight through Elaine's head and made her ears tingle. Almost immediately it came – a soft, scurrying, scuttling noise. Elaine looked around in surprise. It seemed as if

the walls, the inside of the roof, the very floor were moving in waves towards her. Then Elaine realised what it was.

Thousands and millions and *trillions* of spiders.

"Hhmm, hhmm!" Vinegar cleared her throat for silence. "Hello, friends. Elaine here needs our help to find her granma's ring. She's been switched with Jolly the spiteful until she finds it. Will you all help?"

"But of course . . . "

"Naturally . . . "

"Certainly . . . "

The attic was filled with the noise of a zillion spiders all agreeing very politely to help.

"Your turn, Grimbledon," Vinegar said.

"We'd better come out of the attic. There isn't room in here for your friends *and* mine," said Grimbledon.

So Elaine, Grimbledon and Vinegar walked out of the attic followed by a zillion, sprillion spiders. Once they reached the top of the steps which led down to the first floor, Grimbledon gave three low, long, loud whistles which shot straight

through Elaine's head and made her ears jingle.

At once there came a rumbling and a tumbling and a pitter-patting which seemed to echo throughout the entire house.

Up the stairs they came. What seemed to Elaine like every mouse in the world.

51

"You lot took your blinkin' time!" Grimbledon said. "Elaine here has got to stay in the body of Jolly the malicious until she finds her granma's ring – and she's only got until tomorrow dinner-time to do it. Are we going to help Elaine or are we going to allow Jolly the repulsive to gloat over Elaine forever?"

"No bloomin' fear . . . "

"Never . . . "

"We'll help you Elaine . . . " came an assortment of squeaks and squeals from the stairs.

"Thank you all," Elaine said, choked. "Between all of us we should find Granma's ring with no problems."

"Not so fast my prrrretty one. I think you've forrrrgotten about me," came a voice from the bottom of the stairs.

It was Jolly, in Elaine's body.

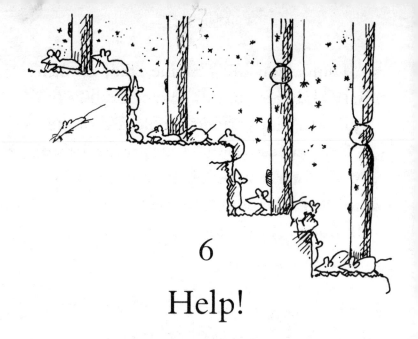

6

Help!

THE MICE SHRIEKED AND RAN scampering up the stairs whilst the spiders fled up the walls behind Elaine.

"Have you come to help me too?" Elaine asked.

"You must be blinkin' joking, Elaine," snorted Grimbledon.

"My dear girl, surely you jest!" Vinegar shook her head.

At the foot of the stairs, Jolly growled

with laughter. "Me! Help you! I like being a girrrrl. I don't want to be a cat again."

"But that's my body," Elaine protested.

"It's mine now and I'm going to make surrrre that I keep it," Jolly purred.

"My friends and I won't let you," said Elaine confidently.

"Yourrrr frrrriends?" Jolly laughed. "I'll show you what I think of yourrrr frrrriends."

Jolly dashed up the stairs after the fleeing mice. Faster than fast, her hand swooped down to catch the tail of the last mouse still scampering away. Jolly lifted the mouse over her mouth and dangled it there.

"Laddle-luggens!" Grimbledon shouted out, dashing down the stairs.

"Yourrrr name is Laddle-luggens is it?" Jolly said to the wriggling-jiggling mouse in her grasp.

"Help! Help!" squeaked Laddle-luggens.

"Well, Laddle-luggens, you look like a tasty morrrrsel," said Jolly, licking her lips.

"You mean, evil, rotten cat. Put him down," Elaine shouted.

"I'm not a cat. I'm a girrrrl now," Jolly said. "But I think the occasional mouse now and then would be a perrrrfect trrrreat."

Elaine dashed down the stairs after Grimbledon just as Jolly opened her mouth to swallow Laddle-luggens whole.

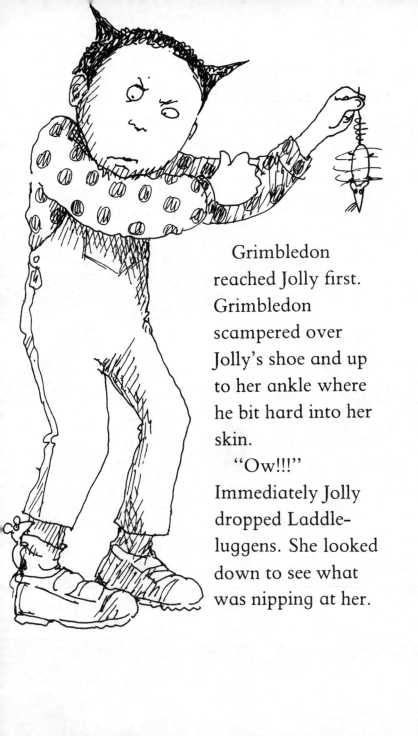

Grimbledon reached Jolly first. Grimbledon scampered over Jolly's shoe and up to her ankle where he bit hard into her skin.

"Ow!!!" Immediately Jolly dropped Laddle-luggens. She looked down to see what was nipping at her.

Elaine caught Laddle-luggens in her
mouth by his tail as he fell. She scampered
up the stairs with him, releasing him once
she had reached the attic. Then she turned
and ran down the stairs to help Grimbledon. Jolly was furious. She was swiping
again and again for Grimbledon who
darted and weaved between her legs.

"You leave him alone," Elaine said furiously, launching herself at Jolly's skirt. "Run Grimbledon, run!"

Even though Jolly was a girl now she still spitted and snarled like an angry cat.

Elaine released Jolly's skirt and dashed up the stairs after Grimbledon.

"Run my prrrecious, run," Jolly called after her. "But it won't do you any good.

You won't find yourrrr grrrranma's rrrring and even if you do I won't let you give it to herrrr."

"You can't stop me," Elaine said from the top of the stairs.

"Can't I? We'll see about that my prrr-retty," hissed Jolly, and off she strode.

Elaine, Grimbledon, Vinegar and all the friends searched throughout the house all night. They searched in the attic, they searched through all the rooms on the first floor, they searched through all the rooms on the ground floor, they searched through the basement.

They found forgotten books and thrown-away hooks. They found a broken watch and an ink stain splotch. They found a big, blue box and some smelly socks. They found practically everything – *except* Granma's ring.

The morning sun began to rise in the sky and soon it was shining bright and warm. When at last they had all gathered together by the back door of the house, Elaine, took one look at all the miserable faces and knew that the ring still hadn't been found.

Just then Elaine heard Granma's light, sprightly step on the stairs above them. Turning her head, Elaine saw her granma coming down towards them.

And there behind her was Jolly. Elaine unsheathed her claws and stretched them out, ready if Jolly should try something else.

"Elaine, I'm glad you've found some friends to help you," Granma said. Granma smiled as she looked around at all the mice and spiders. Granma looked relieved to see Elaine had help. Elaine shook her head at the thought. She must be imagining things.

"Oh, Granma, *please*. You've got to

change me back," Elaine pleaded. "We've searched and *searched* and we haven't been able to find it."

"Elaine dear, I've already explained. Only you can break the spell by finding my ring and giving it back to me." Granma sniffed and took off her spectacles to polish them. "I wish I could help you. I really do."

Elaine's heart fell all the way down to the

end of her tail when she heard that. The ring had to be somewhere. Maybe there was some place they had all missed? Elaine glanced past Granma to see Jolly smirking at her.

'Right! I'll soon get rid of that smile,' Elaine thought angrily.

"Granma, I've got something to tell you about Jolly . . ." Elaine began.

"Elaine's going to tell you about how I offerrrred to help herrrr," Jolly interrupted. "I asked herrrr not to tell you but I guess she thought you should know."

Granma put back on her spectacles.

"Now, Elaine," she said, peering at Elaine over them, "why on earth shouldn't you tell me that Jolly offered to help you? Well done, Jolly. That was very kind of you. If we all work at it, we're bound to find it. And I'm glad to see you're all getting on so well."

Elaine stared at Jolly. Of all the bare-faced lies Elaine had ever heard that one was the barest and the boldest. Elaine wasn't the only one who was speechless either. All her friends were glaring and staring and glowering and scowling at Jolly too.

"Well, I'll leave you all to it," Granma smiled kindly. "Don't forget Elaine, you only have until dinner-time to get my ring back to me. Good luck."

"Granma wait . . ." Elaine began, but it was too late. Granma had disappeared back up the stairs.

Elaine stretched out her claws even further as she watched Jolly.

"You lying toad!" Elaine hissed.

"Now, now. Is that any way to talk to the cat who's now got yourrrr body?" Jolly grinned.

"Not for much longer," Elaine retorted.

"But you've searrrrched the whole house and you haven't found the rrrring. And if it has anything to do with me, you neverrrr will," Jolly said, her smile disappearing to be replaced with a nasty sneer.

And with that Jolly bounded up the stairs, without looking back once. Elaine watched Jolly go. She wanted to shout out to Jolly that they would find the ring – no problem. But the whole house had been searched now and . . . nothing.

"I'm going to be a cat forever," Elaine said slowly and lay down with her head on her front paws.

"Nonsense dear," Vinegar said briskly. "You're not going to let Jolly the odious beat you, are you?"

"But we haven't found the ring," Elaine pointed out. "And there's nowhere else left to search."

And Elaine, all the mice and all the spiders sat in a sad silence, wondering what they could do next.

7

We'll Never Find It

"I'VE GOT IT." VINEGAR'S VOICE WAS so unexpected it made everyone jump. "There's still one place we haven't explored yet. We haven't searched the *garden*."

"The garden!" Grimbledon said excitedly. "I forgot all about that." Elaine sat up. "The garden? But isn't it very big?"

"So blinkin' what? There are plenty of us here. We'll all stretch out in a line and walk from one end of the garden to the other looking for the ring," Grimbledon said confidently.

"There's a well and lots of trees in the garden," Vinegar said, "so we'll search those as well once we've searched through the grass."

"Why do we need to search the trees? Granma's ring won't be up in one of those!" Elaine said.

"You never know, dear," Vinegar said.

"A blinkin' bird may have carried it up into a tree for all we know," Grimbledon said.

So out they all went into the garden.

The mice and spiders lined up against the outside wall of the house, standing foot to foot to foot to foot . . .

More mice and spiders stood in front of them and more still in front of *them*, so that if the first line missed the ring then the second line would not and even if they did,

the third line was bound to spot it.

"Okay, friends, stay alert," ordered Vinegar.

"Keep your blinkin' eyes peeled, everyone," piped up Grimbledon.

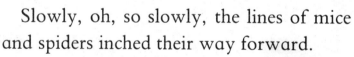

Slowly, oh, so slowly, the lines of mice and spiders inched their way forward.

The sun was well up in the sky before they had even covered half of the garden. And the sun had begun to climb very, very

slowly down again before they had got three-quarters of the way through the grass.

Elaine looked up at the sky, then up at her granma's dining-room window. Elaine knew she had less than an hour left before she was going to be a cat forever. There was still a patch of garden left to search when a few mice and spiders began to mutter and grumble.

"We'll never find this ring . . ."

"This is silly . . ."

"It's a complete waste of time . . ."

Elaine hung her head. She couldn't really blame those mice and spiders who would rather be doing something else. It wasn't a very enjoyable task, sniffing and scratching at the grass and ground to try and find Granma's ring. Her own neck and her eyeballs ached from peering at the ground, intent on not missing the ring and Elaine

was sure that everyone else was as tired as
she was. After all none of them had got any
sleep.

"Listen everyone," Elaine called out. "I . . .
I know that some of you are getting fed
up. You . . . you can go if you want to. But I
still want to thank you for helping me . . ."

Vinegar scampered up the wall of the well to stand at the top of it.

"Friends, we can't desert Elaine in her hour of need," Vinegar cried. "Elaine is our friend – we can't let her down. And besides, do you want to see Jolly the loathsome stay in Elaine's body? Is it right that Elaine should remain a cat for the rest of her life? No! NO!"

"Come on mates. Vinegar's right. Elaine needs us," Grimbledon shouted. "Are we going to let her down?"

"No!" everyone shouted.

"Hooray!" Vinegar jumped up and down on top of the well, waving all of her arms and legs at once.

Only she jumped up a little too high and waved her eight arms and legs with a little too much enthusiasm.

SPLOSH! Vinegar fell backwards into the well.

"Vinegar!" Elaine jumped up onto the well wall and peered down into the shadowy water below. "Vinegar, are you all right?"

"Oh dear! What a state! I'm soaked. Yes, dear, I'm all right. I can't believe I was quite that clumsy though. I'm not usually. And the fresh silk I spun only this morning is ruined!"

"How are we going to get you out?" Elaine called down.

"I'll climb out," Vinegar said.

Vinegar placed her arms and legs on the well walls but they immediately slipped off. She tried again but the same thing happened.

"Oh dear, the walls are slippery and slimy," Vinegar said anxiously.

"Can't you climb up?" Elaine asked.

"I can't get a foothold, dear," Vinegar replied. "I'm going to have to tread water for a while."

"But if we leave you down there you'll get tired and then you'll sink into the water and drown," Elaine said horrified.

"Never mind that. Leave me here," Vinegar ordered. "You can't afford to waste time helping me."

"But we can't leave you," Elaine said.

"You're going to have to decide what we should do, Elaine," Grimbledon said. "Whatever you think is best."

"Elaine go!" Vinegar ordered. "If you try to save me, by the time you fish me out it will be dinner-time. If you help me you'll be a cat forever."

8

A Decision to Make

ELAINE LOOKED AT THE MICE AND spiders around her. They were all watching her, waiting for her decision.

Elaine thought hard. They didn't have time to search for the ring *and* rescue Vinegar. They'd have to do one or the other. If they searched for Granma's ring, Vinegar would drown. But if they rescued Vinegar, then Elaine would remain a cat for the rest of her life.

Elaine looked at Grimbledon and all the other mice and she looked at all the spiders who were helping her because Vinegar had asked them to. They were her friends. She'd never had any friends that liked her and helped her before. But when she'd been a girl, she'd been really selfish and only thought about herself.

"Vinegar, hang on. We're going to get you out," Elaine shouted.

"Yeepee!"

"Hooray!"

The garden was
filled with the sound
of all the mice and
spiders cheering.

"Listen everyone,
we'll need some
spiders to form a
ladder down the well
so that Vinegar can
climb up on their
backs," Elaine
shouted. "The spiders
at the top of the well
can hold onto a chain
of mice to make sure
they don't slip."

Within minutes the
spiders were slowly

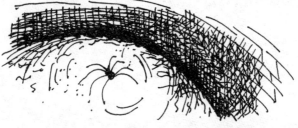

but surely climbing over each other and holding onto each other's arms and legs as they made a ladder down the well. Progress was steady but extremely slow.

"Elaine dear, I'm so sorry," Vinegar called out miserably. "If I hadn't been so clumsy then you wouldn't have to do this."

"Don't be silly," Elaine called down into the well, her voice echoing back at her. "We're not going to leave you down there. Besides, it's smelly."

Elaine wrinkled up her cat nose at the slick, slimy, slithery smell down the well. It smelt like a dustbin full of thrown-away food which had been sitting rotting for ages.

"I'm getting cramp," Vinegar called out, "I'd better swim around for a while."

As Elaine watched, Vinegar began to swim round and round in circles. Suddenly Vinegar screamed.

"I've found it, I've found it."

"Found what?" Elaine peered down into the darkness. "Vinegar are you all right?"

"I've found the ring, your granma's wedding ring. I'vc found it," Vinegar screamed. "It's jammed between two bricks in the wall here. I'll get it out."

"Be careful," Elaine called down.

At last the ladder of spiders reached down to the water.

Trampling and trompling over the other spiders' heads, Vinegar finally made it to the top of the well and stepped out onto the wall, Granma's ring dangling from her mouth.

Vinegar dropped it on the grass by the well. "Gosh, that was heavy." Then slowly and surely the ladder of spiders was pulled up by a chain of mice.

"We've done it. Hooray! We've done it!" Elaine beamed, licking up Granma's ring and putting it under her tongue. "Granma will put me back in my proper body now."

"And not before time either," said Grimbledon. "Look at the sun. It's so low in the sky. We've only got a few minutes."

"And none of you arrrre going anywherrrre," said Jolly from the back door.

"You can't stop us," Grimbledon called out angrily. "One of us will take the ring and get past you. You can't stop all of us."

"*I* can't stop all of you but I have a few frrrriends with me," Jolly said with a sly smile. "Come out. I'm surrrre Elaine and the rrrrest would like to see you."

Cats and more cats appeared from behind Jolly until the door-way was full to overflowing with cats. They climbed up the door frame, they filled the stairs behind Jolly, they stood poised at her feet.

"Let's see any of you get past me *and* my frrrriends," Jolly smirked.

9

Jump!

"WHY, YOU BIG BULLY," VINEGAR fumed.

"You mean, malicious, vile and vicious..."

"Never mind that Grimbledon," Elaine interrupted. "What are we going to do now?"

Elaine looked up at the sky. The sun was very low now and Elaine could see Granma sitting by her open window, just starting her dinner.

"Another ladder," Grimbledon said suddenly. "We need another ladder of mice going up the wall to your granma. Come on everyone. We don't have a moment to lose."

"You'll neverrrr do it in time," Jolly said confidently, crossing her arms in front of her.

Ignoring her, the mice clambered to make a ladder up the wall towards Granma's window.

Anxiously Elaine watched. A whole row of mice stood beneath Granma's window, then more mice got on top of them, then more mice got on top of *them* until the pyramid of mice quickly and steadily grew.

"Come on!
Faster!" Grimbledon
shouted.

The pyramid was
halfway up the wall.
The sun was getting
lower. Elaine chewed
her lip anxiously.
What would happen?

"Quick, Elaine,
start climbing,"
Grimbledon called
out.

Jolly walked out into the garden to see how far the pyramid of mice had got up the wall.

Elaine bounded up the pyramid, climbing higher and higher but trying not to hurt the mice she was stepping on.

"Frrrriends, quick. I need your help," Jolly called. "Elaine is almost at herrrr grrrranma's window."

The mice climbed up faster to build the pyramid higher. Elaine was only a metre away from her granma's open window.

"Get them! Get them!" Jolly hissed, tearing at the pyramid of mice. The pyramid began to sway, then to rock as Jolly pulled mice away from it.
Elaine looked up at her granma's window. So near and yet so far.

"Jump, Elaine, jump," Grimbledon shouted.

"I can't jump that far," Elaine called back desperately.

"Elaine dear – JUMP!" Vinegar shouted. "The pyramid is about to collapse."

Elaine sat back and with one bound she leapt towards the window, her paws outstretched. She sailed through the air . . . She wasn't going to make it . . . Stretching out further than she'd thought possible, Elaine grabbed for the window sill. She made it! Using her back legs to push against the wall, she leapt through the window right into Granma's lap. Elaine spat out the ring into her gran's lap, just as Granma put down her dessert spoon.

"My wedding ring!" Granma said. "Oh, well done, Elaine, well done. I was hoping you'd find it, not because I wanted it back but because I wanted *you* back. Mind you, you cut it rather fine, dear. Another five seconds and you would have been a cat forever."

"Will you change me back now?" Elaine asked.

"Of course I will. Jump down off my lap and as soon as your feet touch the carpet you'll be a girl again."

Elaine jumped down. Immediately she ran to the window.

"Granma, please do something. Your cat Jolly is hurting my friends. They helped me find your ring and now Jolly is mad at them because she wanted to stay a girl."

With a frown Granma got up and went to the window. The garden was full of cats chasing mice and spiders and right in the middle of them was Jolly, back in her proper body, once again a cat.

"Jolly, what do you think you're doing?" Granma called out sternly. Instantly, all the cats were frozen to the spot. But only the cats. The mice and spiders dashed as far away from the cats as they could get,

crowding under Granma's window. Jolly looked up at Granma.

"Miaow! Miaow!"

Elaine listened hard but she could no longer understand what Jolly was saying.

"Don't lie, madam," Granma said angrily. "I see I have been seriously fooled by you. You are not the cat I thought you were, Jolly."

"Miaow! Miaow! Mia-ow!"

"I don't believe you," Granma replied. "Now if you want to be welcomed back into this house you will leave Elaine's friends alone. If you or your friends have hurt even one of them, then you can look for a new place to live."

"Mia-ow! Mia-ow!

Elaine wished she could still understand what Jolly was saying. As Elaine watched, Jolly's friends slunk off, climbing up the garden fence and running away.

"The idea! I've never seen such behaviour," Granma muttered. "I shall have to keep a very close eye on that cat."

With her head bent, Jolly walked through the crowds of mice and spiders and into the house.

Then the mice and spiders crowded underneath the window, filling the air with squeaks and scuttling noises.

"Your friends are saying congratulations," Granma told Elaine.

"I can't understand them any more," Elaine said sadly.

"Of course you can. Just listen with your heart, not your ears." Elaine looked out of the window at her friends. She saw Grimbledon and next to him was Vinegar.

"Thank you all," Elaine said, tears of happiness in her eyes. "You were my first friends and I'll never forget you. And if Jolly tries to bully any of you, you must let me or my granma know."

Elaine listened carefully.

"Bye, Elaine," Grimbledon shouted.

"Goodbye, Elaine dear," Vinegar said.

And the mice and spiders scurried in all directions until the garden was empty.

Elaine turned to her granma.

"Granma, I'm sorry I was so rude to you," Elaine said.

"And I'm sorry I lost my temper," Granma said. "Do you forgive me?"

Elaine nodded.

"Now then, I have some news for you. Your dad went for an interview for another job a couple of weeks ago and today he found out that he got it. He wanted to tell you himself but you wouldn't give him a chance," Granma said.

"What's his new job?" Elaine asked.

Hope, like a light being switched on, suddenly appeared inside her. Elaine crossed her fingers hard. The hardest she had ever done in her life.

"He's going to be the manager in charge of selling computers in this area. So when he gets back you and he are both going to live with me. We're all going to share this

house – but only if you want to."

"Oh Granma . . ."

"And of course that means that you'll be able to go to the local school as well," Granma said. "You'll be able to make some real, lasting friends. There will be no more travelling."

No more trips abroad, except for holidays. Elaine couldn't believe it.

"Oh, Granma, I'd love that more than anything," Elaine grinned. And Elaine and her granma hugged each other.